EYEWITNESS

a Novella

by John C. Connell

Acknowledgments

Thank you Jesus, for this story idea and inspiration (among many other things!). Thanks always to my wife and family for their continual support. Special thanks also to Michele Hocking for her critical eye and generosity.

Dedication

For Lori

Prologue

Dreaming only in sound may seem strange to you, but for the first twenty-eight years of my life, it was all I ever knew. I often wondered what it would be like to *see* my dreams, when hearing others speak of their experiences. Then after it started happening, I realized you can't pick and choose what you see. Even worse, I learned some visions just stay with you whether you're asleep or awake.

The one that haunts and taunts me like a shadow, is of the *Son of Man*, my Sight Giver: shaking, bleeding, twisting and wincing on an inhumane pedestal. He eventually found me in the crowd. He can appear whenever I close my eyes. He sees me through his own swollen eyelids and looks deep into my very soul.

- 1 -

Ping. That unmistakable chime of coin hitting stone led me to reach out with caution to my left. Within a moment, I captured my treasure and snapped back for fear of being stepped on. There is nothing like reading the ground in front of you with your hands and coming under foot. The sharp, biting pain of a well-placed sandal is something you can never plan for, or get used to.

I amused myself by referring to that Sabbath day as "bath day". Hot and humid bath day. It was late in the year, and the heat was a surprise. I think the entire city brushed and pressed against me as it hustled and bustled around the Pool of Siloam.

Ritual washing tapered off in cooler conditions. Sensing a seasonal change was just around the corner, everyone was out. This would be the largest crowd for a while, until the annual, winter's Feast of the Dedication. The buzz of the courtyard, filled with many voices and smells, kept my mind and ears alert.

I am blind.

The weight and feel of the new piece I picked up told me it was silver. Someone felt generous, which was a rarity anymore. Adding it to the few copper kodrantes in my lap brought the total up just enough to give me hope for the afternoon.

"There you go." A voice jumped from the crowd at me as something tapped my toe. Whoa, the day was shaping up! I investigated, only to find a greasy bone from some glutton. No doubt the culprit was Roman. I can still hear the laughter that faded back into the crowd along with the men who used me as their trash gutter.

I strained my dead eyes. I could see in my own way. I tried to "picture" sounds in my head. Sounds have their own shapes. Craning my neck in the direction of that laughter, I was desperate to stand and throw that bone back to its donor, stand and let everyone know that I would not be...well, it was no use.

I could hear my mother like always, speaking to me from deep inside my mind, reminding me that I was born blind and there was nothing I could do about it. I just had to accept my lot in life. Curse my lot, Mother!

I dropped the bone to my right and was quick to wipe my fingers on my hip. I had to get rid of the Roman's residue before I caught something. Hanging my head in self-pity, and resisting the urge to smell my fingers, I could feel the attention of those around me. *Look at the poor blind man reach for what he thought was money. HA!*

Home suddenly seemed like a much better place to be. My ear listened over my left shoulder, as if to hear my corner of the house calling me to safety. Enjoying the thought and temptation to leave, without assistance, helped erase the embarrassment.

Begging for money was my official reason for being there. It was important to my father that I "do my part" to contribute to the family's well being. Even on the Sabbath. Father didn't think the law applied to people like me.

I settled down and tried to ignore the rhythms of people's sandals. There were plenty of them around me. The sounds that travelers made could tell entire stories.

Soon the sun felt like it was parked just a couple feet above my head, and left me wiping sweat off the sides of my face and neck. The heat burned off both my energy and patience.

Numbness moved around my legs. My throat felt like a rocky, dry road and I couldn't make any spit to swallow. The sounds of those in the water were antagonistic. I fought the urge to just cover my ears, to try and block it all out.

It wasn't just sounds I wanted to block out. There were comments too. Insults. I was blind, not deaf.

A woman called out, presumably to a child, "Get over here. Stay away from him." People could be so callous. It was apparent she considered my presence a danger.

Then two men, standing over my spot, spoke about me like I was a goat or calf. "Wonder what his father's great sin was?"

"Maybe his mother's the trouble."

They chuckled and I fought the urge to kick and trip.

I sat against a wall, the same wall I held up for years. I knew it angled away from me off to my left. I thought I could stand and feel my way, like at home, around the yard until the wall stopped. After that came a high traffic street that would be more difficult to navigate.

There were rough roads that led to my home. There were also curves and alleys that could throw me off course. I most surely would become lost. Some people would take pity on me and help. Some people would not. What if I ran into the kind of men that throw bones at blind people? What if I stumbled into a group of Romans?

And so I stayed, steaming under my tunic, which was heavy with perspiration.

"What now, Lord?" I asked aloud. It wasn't very loud but I didn't go out of my way to whisper, either. It didn't matter. No one was listening to me anyway.

I thought of some lines from a few Psalms I knew, but couldn't decide which to pray. I didn't really want to pray them anyway. I really only wanted to ask Him--. The rest of my thought vanished.

I became aware that I was being observed.

Not the way most people observed me: where they looked down as they passed and either made a comment or searched their purse for a donation. No. I felt I was being watched. Watched and *discussed*.

I was convinced it was my two brothers. They had this annoying habit of standing a ways away from me, trying to get a look at the day's collection. Based on how much they thought I earned (I use that term loosely) while they were gone, I would be retrieved for home, or let sit a while longer. Like everyone else, they seemed to think that because I was blind, the rest of my senses were also worthless. Complete fools!

My spirit rose with the prospect of a trip home. I wanted to yell in their direction to quit debating already and take me. I chewed on my tongue while deciding what to do. Impatience won out.

I raised my head and started to open my mouth but closed it again. I heard a voice that didn't belong to one of my brothers.

The next sound I heard was the slight shifting of the gravel directly in front of me. Someone was hovering over me. I was sure of it.

I lifted and tilted my head at the sound, trying to "see" my visitor with my ears. I listened closely for more sounds -- his sounds -- to try and hear the story they told about him, but he stood so still.

The voice I didn't recognize came again from a short distance away. "Rabbi", it called, but received no response. I became aware that a few of the conversations in my vicinity trailed off. I wasn't the only one intrigued with this newcomer.

"Is that him?" a voice to my right muttered.

"Yes, I think it is", another whispered.

Dirt and gravel shifted again. I could feel my visitor getting closer. He may have even crouched down to my level. I was sure that I could have reached out and touched him, but I didn't. Why, I don't know. I didn't move at all. I just kept trying to listen.

I could still hear splashing from the pool mixed with the crowd's hum in the background, but there seemed to be a small and growing radius of quiet around us.

Something wet landed on my right arm and I heard soft slapping sounds, like the first droplets of a shower on hard, dusty rock.

A rhythm emerged from those slapping sounds. The odd and silent one was patting the ground in front of me.

My memory clouds a bit after that, but I can still hear those slapping sounds in the back of my head. They're there forever now, in the same place my mother's voice was when I heard her reminding me of my lot in life.

But other than that, all I remember is pain. A pain I never ever felt before, because it was in my eyes.

- 2 -

My hands flew to my face when the burning started. I felt something slimy on my eyelids and rubbed and scratched at it, but my skin continued to grow hotter. My cheeks and forehead flushed and radiated heat. I shook my head back and forth as my confusion raced towards fear.

I must have cried out or done something to draw attention to myself because the quiet that surrounded me moments before was gone. There was movement and scuffling sandals and hands touching me. Someone grabbed me under my arms and was trying to haul me to my feet. My own hands were still fused to my face, my fingertips digging into my skull.

12

I straightened up, attempting to stand under my own power, and I heard a booming voice next to me. A deep, lucid voice rang out in my right ear that I knew even then, though I could not see, came from the stranger who had started the trauma. He leveled a single command at me to go and wash off in the pool.

I floundered to my right; the direction I thought led to the bath of Siloam. My shoulder rammed hard into the wall I had been sitting against. My left hand struck the face of the man I believe was responsible for getting me to my feet. I was twisted around and disoriented. My balance slid away from me and I slid back down the wall towards the ground.

A pair of strong arms slipped themselves around my waist and pulled me away from the wall. My feet took off to catch my body and my arms flailed out in front of me. My sense of direction was now completely absent. My right foot kicked something hard and the pain that had wrapped itself around my head jumped to my foot.

My knees buckled and my momentum caused me to fall forward. Putting my arms out in front of me, I somehow managed to land on my chest and elbows, keeping my head from bouncing off the pool's descending steps, which were carved into the surrounding rock.

I slithered forward on my knees, reaching out with every bit of my length to find the water's edge. Suddenly, cool droplets jumped out to greet me. Water was being thrown, splashed towards me. The hands that were around my waist were now on my back, trying to force me closer to the water. My legs pushed off the cut rock steps and my left hand broke the water's surface. I plunged forward, out of my helper's grasp and slammed into the pool.

I beat my face under water, convinced the muck on my eyelids was generating all the pain. In my zeal I inhaled water. My throat seized, my body shuddered and convulsed. I planted my feet on the pool's shallow bottom and stood up from under the water with the same force I had used to throw myself into it.

Vomiting water, I coughed and gagged. The pain in my face vanished – for a moment. I felt dizzy. My head buzzed and tingled and I stumbled a bit in the water. A woman gasped at that and I could feel things getting quiet again.

I rubbed the left side of my head, feeling my ear and tried to touch something else, something that felt like it was inside my head, something new.

I held my head in my hands and that was when the real terror began.

- 3 -

The pain came back in waves this time, like a succession of daggers piercing my mind. My hands ran all over my face and found no trace of that foreign substance. My skin no longer burned but my head throbbed. The pain had found a way in.

Even today I find it hard to verbalize what it was like. I have never been able to find the right words to convey that moment. The moment when I started to realize what was happening, what was *really* happening. Anyone I try to tell can't comprehend it. They can't fathom how something they have experienced from birth could be so frightening.

As I stood there with my hands pressed tightly over my eyes, coughing, drooling, and swooning in the water, I screamed. The stabbing pain was accompanied by something else, something I didn't know existed, and something I found terrifying.

Light.

Every time I moved a hand or blinked, it was there. You cannot understand. *I* could not understand after all those years in darkness, only seeing in shades of black. My body tried to reject the light but it wouldn't go away. It was in all directions. I still didn't know that I was seeing at that point. My heart galloped in my chest as I continued to rub my eyelids. I would blink madly and then clamp my eyes shut again because that pain-filled light was still there.

Then the truth started to take hold of me. The light danced around my hands, trying to find its way to my eyes. Wonder and horror collided inside of me as I realized I was actually *seeing* my hands. I perceived the shapes of my fingertips. I started to link together the images of movement with the sensations of my fingers tapping my face.

It must have been several minutes before I started to make out other shapes and motions. I just kept standing there, staring into my hands. My vision was blurry but I didn't know that at the time.

I found that by just barely cracking my eyes open, in effect looking through my eyelashes, I could tolerate the pain brought by the light. Slowly, I would bring my hands away from my face and move my fingers. I had to close my eyes every minute or so for just a few seconds. I had to retreat back into the darkness to get my bearings.

My ears re-opened and I started to recognize the familiar buzzing of the crowd and the various sounds of the pool water all around me. I also started to feel the rest of my body, statue stiff and exhausted.

It occurred to me all at once that if I could make out my hands, I could make out other things. I looked down and pulled my hands far enough away from my head to venture a look at myself. There I was, at least the part of me that I could see.

I could only make out my tunic-covered torso before sealing my eyes shut again. That hurtful light was everywhere, bouncing and flickering. I kept my left hand clamped over my eyes while my right hand ran down my chest and over my stomach. All the while I was gathering up my strength and forcing myself to dare another peek.

Slowly, one glimpse turned into two, then four, then too many to recount. Each one was short however, because of the sunlight. It was reflected off the surrounding water. I didn't realize, of course, that water was reflective. That, and so much more, came to me in time. In those moments I thought the pool itself was the source of the light.

With eyes closed, I dragged my right hand through the water. I cracked my eyelids open enough to see my hand make a small wave. I did that again and again in total amazement. Feeling the water and then seeing what it felt like. Each time looking for as long as I could without shutting my eyes to reconnect with my borderless, lightless comfort zone.

"...all right?!"

My head snapped to attention. Someone was close and trying to talk to me. Before I could respond he spoke again. Louder. "Are you all right?!"

I forced my eyes open and almost screamed again. I could see him standing there at the pool's edge. He was leaning toward me.

For however long I was in the water trying to get acclimated to my new ability, it hadn't occurred to me that I would be able to see other people. The sight of this man, leaning over the edge of the water, one hand outstretched, introduced me to the world at large.

With eyes shut again, my mind raced away from him, trying to gather up a list of what was out there to be seen. The courtyard, the crowd, the rest of the city, my...my brothers, and parents, my home!

I suddenly couldn't feel the rest of my body. The scope of this was all too much. I needed to rest, to sleep, undisturbed in darkness for about...

The man's hand yanked me back to the courtyard, to the pool, to him, and to the light. I blinked rapidly and caught the sight of his hand fastened to my forearm, anchoring me to him and the rest of the world. He was still speaking to me.

"...with me, you'll be just fine. Come. I'll get you up and out of the water."

To this day, when remembering that man, I picture how his mouth moved as he spoke. His jaw just bobbed back and forth as the words came out. His lips wrinkled and smoothed. I had felt people's faces before, many times, as well as my own, so I was aware that happened when you spoke. But to see it happen was, well, unforgettable.

The man then took hold of me with both hands and leaned closer to me. His voice tried to assure me that I was going to be just fine, but I didn't believe him. He gently started to pull me towards him and the edge of the pool. I was still blinking at that point and my eyes were bouncing back and forth between the moving water and his arms. I felt unsure of my footing and closed my eyes to find my equilibrium. I kept them closed and gladly relied upon the darkness and my other senses to center me, to guide me.

With my hands and one of my feet I felt the edge of the pool, a stone riser leading to a step. It felt safe and cool. I cracked my eyes to get a look at it. It was darker than the water and didn't hurt as bad to focus on. My hands were on the stone as the man, still unaware of my new ability, tried to guide me out.

He said something about lifting a leg out onto the stones and then proceeded to quickly raise an arm to my shoulder. I happened to blink again at that moment, trying to get another look at his moving mouth, and saw his hand flying up towards me. I snapped back and put my own hands to my face in defense.

I held my hands there for a moment before peeking out through my fingers. He was staring at me. The expression on his face, I would come to learn, was one of total dismay. It was an expression I would see many times in the days that followed. I closed my eyes again and just started moving forward by feel. I threw a leg out of the water, then the other, and then felt around with my hands before sitting.

I sat for a moment and just listened to my surroundings, and that felt good. I started blinking again. This time, I found myself looking at my sandaled feet. It was the first time I ever saw my toes.

I shut out the rest of the world and stared in awe at my wiggling toes. The man who helped me out of the pool was now crouching down next to me. I could see his feet too. I didn't look up to see the rest of him.

He startled me once more by putting his hand up to me, this time right up to my face. Again I repeated that same defensive motion. A moment later I opened my eyes to see him still waving his hand at me. I waved him off that time and heard him gasp.

He backed off then, mumbling something under his breath. I looked back down to see my right hand fumbling with the leather strapping on one of my sandals.

"You can see me," he said in a loud whisper. "You can see me." I didn't speak. His words were as heavy as my wet clothing. He repeated himself with a little more force. "You can see me!"

The tone was accusatory and I suddenly felt very self-conscious. I continued to look down at my feet, not wanting to interact anymore with that person, not wanting to interact anymore with that whole place.

He persisted. "You can see me, can't you? I know you can see me."

I became aware of the commotion I was destined to create, and started to nod, my eyes never leaving my feet. From somewhere deep

20

inside my gut welled up the response he was searching for. I remember feeling my own jaw move as I spoke. "Yes...I can *see* you."

- 4 -

He left me at that point, tripping over himself as he called out to his friends and anyone else who would listen. Conversations halted and questions flew about, like birds exiting a tree. Many started to wander my way. Several other sandal-clad feet surrounded mine and a few of the gatherers crouched down to get a closer look at me. Whatever happened to me must have been catching, for suddenly a great many people seemed affected by it.

About this time a small herd of clouds trotted past the sun, diminishing its intensity. As the many strangers clustered around me, I could start to make out better detail. My vision began to sharpen.

My head tingled all over as if it were waking from a nap. I started to pan my head back and forth, eyes open, while grasping the ground with both hands for stability. Seeing my 'field' of vision as my head rotated was uncomfortable and difficult to get used to. My stomach bobbed and I again closed my eyes to settle myself.

That took some time because the light now stayed in my head. I closed my eyes and for a moment, still saw brightness before the dark would reclaim its kingdom behind my eyelids.

When I dared to look up, I saw the crowd pressing in on me. Many men were speaking to me at once and I couldn't decipher what any of them were saying. I was desperate to leave. Those feelings of frustration I felt before were back with renewed strength.

What didn't occur to me though, was that, unlike before, I now had the ability to do what I had longed for, to stand and simply walk away.

I looked back down at my hands, still clutching the earth. My fingertips were digging into the ground with the same veracity they had applied to my brow moments before. The many pairs of legs and feet that made up a makeshift prison cell were encroaching upon me. As the crowd jostled about, one man fell forward, almost on top of me and I cowered under him.

Strange, dark shapes moved all over the ground. I noticed them even sliding over my hands. In the days that followed, I would come to know these phenomena quite well, but that afternoon, my first encounter with shadows only added to the hysteria. My mouth opened but no more screams burst out. I was too busy gasping for air.

That was enough! The time came to move on, to leave that madness. I didn't know how I would accomplish it but I got started, nonetheless. Sliding on my backside, I pushed away with my hands and began my retreat from the chaos, my personal exodus. I didn't get very far before I dropped down a step leading back to the pool. I felt cornered as I looked up to see my curious and agitated group of fanatics following.

There was no way I was going to end up back in that water. I couldn't even bring myself to glance at it again. Only one choice remained. I stood.

Eyes closed and head down, I leaned forward and took that first big step. I almost lost my balance when I didn't hit the wall of people I expected to. They moved for me. I felt them all around me. My hands were outstretched in a fashion that was second nature for me. My fingertips lightly touched shoulders and beards and cloaks and other hands.

Afraid of losing the momentum my legs created, I kept walking. After another couple of steps I dared a quick look. Several pairs of hands were being thrust up at me. Some members of the crowd were trying to get my attention. Others were just playing out their skepticism by seeing if I would flinch.

I laid a lot of their questions to rest by not only flinching, but also swatting back at them. My attempts to defend myself only caused greater commotion. Still, I kept moving forward, determined to shed the mob.

I struggled to keep my eyes *open* at that point. I had to use them. Even with so much going on around me that I could not grasp, like depth and color, I was stuck and had to rely upon them!

I didn't think I could do it. I had to remind myself to breathe. My legs felt soft and uncoordinated. I thought I would fall and drown right there in that pool of men.

I raised my head and opened my mouth for what I thought would be my last gasp before going under, when I saw *Him*. He stood directly ahead of me, how far away I had no capacity to determine.

It was really just his face that grabbed me. I don't remember what he was wearing or how tall he was. But something about his eyes stopped me cold. He was an island of calm in that sweltering, chattering storm of people.

I'd like to tell you that I knew right away who he was. But the truth is I only suspected. It wasn't just the way he was looking at me; it was the way he was looking at all of us. He wore the face of understanding. There were no questions in his look, no searching. I think that's what made him instantly stand out to me. He appeared to be the only person that really knew what was going on.

It struck me later that night, as I lay awake in my home, staring out a window and up at the sky's many lights. Lying there, afraid to close my eyes and lose the great gift I was given, it came to me what it was about his gaze that captured my attention. It held the strength I was lacking. Nothing could interrupt his stare. The pushing, pulling, obnoxious crowd didn't bother him. The heat didn't distract him. The light couldn't make him squint.

Back in that maze of men, something in me stirred when I saw him and I leaned forward, pressing further into the herd of onlookers. I wanted to get to where he was, wanted a little of his calm and comprehension. The ground felt a little more solid. I thought it wouldn't be long before I reached him.

It was about then that two strong hands attached themselves to my shoulders and whirled me around in the opposite direction.

- 5 -

"So who was it?" the skinny one queried in an exasperated tone.

It dawned on me that I must have been rambling again. That happened when I got hold of eager ears. The anxiety I felt over meeting the Pharisees when I woke came back. My throat suddenly seemed dry and I sort of bleated a reply, "Who?"

"Yeah, who!?! Who was it that turned you around?" Exasperation was giving way to anger. The skinny man was now leaning out of his chair and his arms were darting up and down to punctuate his speech. He spoke both fast and loud. To his right, a heavy-set man leaned back and thoughtfully tapped his chin with a pudgy but well manicured finger. His eyes were cool and calculating. They never left me.

Next to the large one sat another Pharisee, clearly older than the rest, with bushy, salty eyebrows and beard. He seemed alarmed at the skinny one's agitated state but said nothing. He listened intently to my story. At times, his eyes widened and I thought I saw sincere questions flicker in them.

The last of the four in the room was young enough to pass for the elder's grandson. He rarely acknowledged me, for he was reading some scrolls opened on a table. As I spoke he continually thumbed through his materials. It was as if he was trying to locate something in particular, before the meeting ended.

"My...my brother. My brothers had returned to the pool and pushed their way through the crowd to reach me."

I opened my mouth to add something when the large one cut me off. "So what did this Jesus say to you?" The thin one's head and neck snapped in my direction. He leaned so far out of his chair I thought he would topple to the floor.

I felt my throat closing. My voice wanted to hide. I could sense their displeasure with me, and my responses. "Just... to go and wash my face off in the pool."

"No, no. What else did he say? When you went back to him."

"I, I never made it to him. My brothers guided me home."

"So since you haven't spoken to him, how did you know what he used on your face?"

"From others who were there, sir. We have had a steady stream of visitors at our ho-"

The large one waved off my words with one of his heavy paws. He was about to say something else when the elder, to his right, stopped him short by clearing his throat. The sound immediately earned everyone's attention.

The older man slowly rose from his perch and took three steps towards the back of the room. His eyes signaled the others to follow. The youngest one finally took his nose from the text he was studying and got up. The thin one sprung from his chair and was immediately at the side of the older man. The heavy one stood with more of a concerted effort and took his sweet time shuffling back towards the others.

They spoke for only a few moments. The old man addressed each one of his colleagues individually. When he got to the thin one, he pointed at him. The thin man was taller and looked down at the elder's finger, which was cocked upwards at him. As the older one spoke barely above a whisper, the thinner one shook his head a couple of times in short twitch-like movements. Clearly, they were at odds about something. I then heard the thin one hiss a response, "but he did it on the Sabbath." His elder just held up a hand to stop him.

They came back to the table and the heavy-set Pharisee posed just one last question to me. It was delivered slowly and evenly. "What do you have to say about Jesus since he opened your eyes?"

In the pause that followed, the gates of understanding swung wide open. I had filled myself with worry for nothing! Their interest in me only went as far as my limited association with a man who, for reasons I still didn't understand, did something wonderful for me...I mean *to* me.

I could hear my father's warnings in my head. He was afraid of these men, as was I until just then, for they knew the law - and could ruin those who broke it. My father kept telling me to watch what I say, to just answer their questions and "nothing more."

The fact remained that I hadn't spoken to this man named Jesus. I only knew what others said about him. Healer, teacher, troublemaker, and sinner were the words most often used to describe him. Debates were common when he was brought up. He seemed familiar to the whole city, a familiar stranger.

The one thing I did know for certain was that he was no ordinary man. He was different. But as I stood there I didn't think I could, or should, make that kind of a statement.

So it was a little ironic that when I finally responded to them, I used words from my father, the man who pleaded with me to use as few words as possible. I recalled a conversation I had once with my father when I was just a boy. After hearing him use the word "prophet", I asked him what it was.

He searched for a response, then stated, "Prophets are men of God, who act differently from everybody else, in order to call people's attention to important matters."

The words just came to me and I spoke them with conviction. "He is a prophet."

- 6 -

My stomach told me it was late when my parents returned home. My mother strode into the house and, as if she knew my thoughts, went straight for her jars. The tassels on the train of her cloak brushed the floor between the door and her pantry.

Her eyes avoided mine. At first I only suspected she was averting my gaze. After so many years of never having to meet my eyes, she could have just been acting out of habit. But the sounds of my father banging around outside told me her action was probably intentional.

I couldn't tell what my father was up to outside, but he seemed to be tossing things around in an abrupt manor. The thumps and clangs of whatever he was manhandling were accented by the sweeping sounds of dirt being kicked. He was angry. I could feel it through the walls.

I considered peeking outside to see for the first time what made those familiar sounds. After a few hesitant moments, I decided to not push my luck. Besides, I really wanted to know what upset my parents when they met with the Pharisees. I knew my mother to be a better source of information than my habitually tight-lipped father. I needed to stick close to her.

Many times growing up my brothers generated this type of response from Father, but they weren't here now. The knot inside me said I was at fault, like all those years ago when I left the house one morning to follow my nose. The spring lilies were in bloom.

I learned that day, that exercises of independence were not approved. Independence was proven to be dangerous. The man named Jesus did not seek permission for what he did; he seemed to embrace independence.

I hated feeling out of favor when I was innocent of wrongdoing. How could everyone not be excited? I can *see*. I am no longer living in the dark. A part of me works today that didn't a couple days ago.

Sitting in the corner, contemplating and wrestling with my emotions, I studied my mother as she prepared the supper. Uncovering some leftover bread, she portioned it out amongst the dishes for herself, my father and me. Next she opened the jar containing some of the vegetables she and I acquired yesterday at the marketplace, in between questions from both neighbors and strangers.

Clay receptacles made such interesting ding-like sounds as they were moved around. The bigger the jar, the louder and deeper the sound. Having felt them many times, I could now see what their cool, grainy surfaces looked like.

She left me at that point to go outside and check on our large oven's simmering porridge. The air seemed to clear for the few moments she was gone, and inhaling took less energy.

I closed my eyes and drew in a lung full of aroma from the exposed bread left on the table. It was faint but tantalizing. I began to salivate.

I helped my mother make that bread yesterday after accompanying her to the city. Actually, she made it and I watched. A few times I tried to hand her something she needed, but using my eyes to coordinate movements only slowed her process.

The sound of my mother's distinct walk rhythm, heading back towards the house, grabbed my attention. I reopened my eyes in time to see her enter with a bowl in her arms. The bowl was wrapped in a towel to protect her hands.

Placing the bowl in the center of our family's table, she uncovered it and went back to her vegetable jar. White vapor sailed up from the bowl's contents. My mother called it steam. It was different than the smoke I saw from our oven's fire, but it looked almost the same. I do not understand how supper makes steam but watching its fluid, ever-changing shape put me in a trance.

That spell was broken a couple minutes later. An unidentified male voice spoke to my father, still outside. I leaned back, my head almost touching the wall to hear, but I couldn't make anything out. Whoever my father was speaking with stood too far away.

"Yeah." my father replied. *Yeah to what*, I wondered. He then concluded the conversation, "I'll see to it."

He stepped in the house to find my mother moving towards him. She too was curious. My father held up his hands and walked right past her. She stopped dead in her tracks and let him pass. His gesture said he was not ready to explain.

He stepped over to the wash basin, poured in some water and washed his hands and forearms. I stood up and slowly moved in his direction, watching my feet move me along. By the time I made it across the room, my mother was helping him dry off. He turned towards me, only because I was between him and the table, and walked around me as though he was trying to avoid a post in the middle of the room.

Bending over the basin, I imagined how quiet the house would be if that kind of behavior continued. My hands broke the water's surface. I watched my fingers wiggle as my hands, palms facing up, came to rest on the bottom of the bowl.

I played with the water for another moment until my mother gestured at me with her towel. I raised my arms over the bowl so I could watch the water run down my forearms and drip off my elbows. I tried to follow the drops all the way down into the bowl, fascinated to see them disappear when they hit the rest of the water.

As I dried, my mother splashed water on her hands and arms and took the towel from me. I took my seat at the table and stared into my dish. My father was tearing some bread into ragged sections, and only stopped when my mother finally sat down.

I remained completely still, waiting for my father to say the blessing. He said the same, short prayer of thanks each night. When he still didn't speak, I looked up to find him with his head down, eyes closed and open hands facing the ceiling. After another moment, he jerked his shoulders once, as if he were lifting some invisible thing, and looked at his bread.

I glanced at my mother, who seemed to enjoy complete understanding because she was starting to eat. My father, with a gnarled piece of bread in hand, began sopping up some of the bean porridge from the table's centerpiece.

The aroma from the meal was overpowering my empty stomach and my mouth was wet, but I waited my turn. My father finally broke his silence between his first and second bites. Stabbing at the thickened soup with his bread he announced, "They're going to want to talk to you again!"

- 7 -

Dinner remained awkward until I resigned myself to just keep my head down with eyes only on my food. In doing so I created a level of comfort for my parents – for all of us, really – to operate. Afterwards, my folks loosened enough to even engage in some sporadic conversation.

"So, will you be going tonight?" my mother inquired in her soft way, referring to the nightly neighborhood fire circle, where local men like my father gathered for camaraderie and to share news.

"Oh, I don't know." He muttered through a mouthful.

"You have to sooner or later." She pressed. "I think you'll feel better if you do. You don't want rumors to start."

"I suppose you're right," he determined with a sigh as he rubbed the back of his neck. Mother was right. Everyone at the fire would be waiting to hear from him about his meeting. He didn't have the patience to deal with any speculations and half-truths that his absence might create.

Not long afterwards, he straightened up and left the table while grooming his beard. I took my time finishing my meal. I was content to just let my father ready himself to depart without any additional interactions. My mother picked up the remaining porridge and left the table.

Mother was almost done wiping up after everyone when we heard the familiar whistling of my older brother. Faint and distant at first, the light tones grew closer with their composer. My father left without turning to bid us farewell and met my brother out by the road.

Tension I didn't realize I was carrying around slipped off my shoulders and dropped to the floor. I straightened up and stretched my arms out to their sides before resting my hands on my hips, aware that I had my mother's complete attention for the first time all evening. I closed my eyes and shook my head at the entire situation.

Facing the door my father just walked through, I contemplated how long I could enjoy the reprieve when my mother's hand grasped my shoulder.

"It's a lot for him," she soothed.

What an understatement, I thought. But I let her words hang on me, like the invisible weight I just dropped. "It's a lot for all of us," I countered. "It's the biggest thing that's ever happened to me. And instead of being amazed at this blessing – a blessing no one has ever received before – everyone seems like they would rather it never happened."

Now it was her that let things hang. I turned to face her as I finished my thought. "Everyone except me."

That stung her, and she winced a little. She stared into my eyes and I felt a silent connection, like her person was speaking to me even though her mouth remained closed. Her look said she was sorry. I wondered what she read in my eyes as a reply. I was still learning how much could be said without words.

She was a hand's length shorter than I was, and when we hugged, she stretched her neck to hook her chin up on my shoulder. I smelled her dark hair pressed

against my cheek, and it brought me back to simpler times. I held her there, preferring this side of my mother to the coolness I received earlier.

"It's just that they asked questions we couldn't answer," she said as she let go of me and stepped back.

"I told them everything. I don't understand why they won't listen."

"Won't listen or can't listen? Hopefully this will be over with tomorrow. Your father just wishes he understood what they really wanted," she explained.

I looked past her, toward the window. The shutters were cracked open a bit and I could see the blackness of the night between them. I stated what I thought should be obvious. "They want *him*. Jesus."

I was still staring at the shutters. Soft light bobbed on the walls around the window. The candle nearby flickered from air I could not see. My mother tried to sound reassuring but couldn't because she was the one that needed assurance. "If that's the case, this may all be over in the morning."

I barely heard her. I was fixated on the flickering light. With such amazing things to focus on, how could I care about temple politics?

Mother started to prepare the house for sleep. She pulled out the bedding mattresses from their chest and laid them out on the floor. Hers' and my father's beds were pushed together in the center of the room and mine was slid against the far wall from where I was standing.

I thanked her as I crossed the room but bit my tongue as I realized how fluffy and new my parent's beds were compared to mine. I'm sure they thought that since I couldn't see mine, I would never complain.

Sitting down, I ran my hand along the stitch seam, like so many times before, fingering each little thread. I reclined and fit perfectly into its shape. Looking up at the ceiling, the flickering light from across the room made large dark shadows bob and jump on the support beams. As I watched, I noted that the shadows of things were much less scary than the shadows of men. I became so engrossed in the dance of the shadows that I do not remember my mother readying herself for bed. Their movements seemed liquid, like the steam from our supper, the ripples I made with my hands in the pool of Siloam, or the water in the wash basin before dinner. I let my eyes follow them back and forth, back and forth, until that warm light and those dancing shadows rocked me right to sleep.

Sometime deep in the night, I woke to the raspy brushing sounds of my father's snoring. The house was completely dark. The candle and her shadows had concluded their performance for the evening.

I wondered if I dreamt of Jesus because he was the first person to enter my mind. Where was he at that hour? Where was his home? Who did he help that day? Whose life was changed while the Pharisees interrogated my parents?

I was both angry and amused at the authorities. They did not want me walking around with open eyes, telling my story, yet they desired to hear it again themselves.

My final thought before drifting back to sleep was *they have a real problem on their hands.*

- 8 -

I came fully awake. My parents were up and whispering at the door. Mother was convincing my father of something. The door was partially open and bright shafts of morning were bursting into the room.

I rolled up on one elbow and blinked a few times. It was first time sunlight did not hurt. It was already a better day than I expected.

My father made his way back to me. I sat up straight as he approached.

"Good luck." He wished.

I nodded, "Thank you."

He turned and left for the fields. My father and brothers worked in a vineyard. I couldn't explain what they did, or where the vineyard was, and wondered if I would ever be invited. Whatever the job was, it "kept them young", as he liked to say. Other than the deep, sun-carved cracks in his face, you wouldn't know he was approaching his sixtieth year.

I let a few moments pass before getting up, to let Father make his way down the road. Once on my feet, I made my way to the door. My mother was over by her pantry preparing some food. I didn't notice what kind because I had other matters to tend to.

Emerging from the house in my bare feet, I was surprised to feel how cold the rocky ground was. From inside the sunlight looked warm and encouraging. But the brisk air and chilled path to the latrine proclaimed autumn's arrival.

Standing behind the house I was lost for a few moments, watching my breath. My mouth didn't feel hot but it made steam as though it was the porridge pot from last night. As I returned to the house I questioned my decision to walk around barefoot at this time of year.

My mother's look told me she thought the same thing when I reentered the house. Gesturing to the table, she prodded, "Come and eat something before you go."

A small dish filled with ripe, dark figs sat next to a cup of milk. Figs were my favorite way to start the day. After a quick wash, I grabbed one as I sat and closed my eyes to feel the fruit. The skin had the right amount of give to it. It told me the taste would satisfy my grumbling stomach. I began chewing it whole, including the seeds. It was delicious.

The goat's milk was sweet and rather cool, having just come from our little underground cupboard. I sat content, munching on the figs and staring into my cup, swirling the milk around. I mangled the fruit in my mouth until it turned into a smooth paste before rinsing it down. When I could see most of my plate I stopped eating and drinking and just played instead, watching the milk ripple and smooth from even the slightest vibration. I also liked to tip my cup to watch the creamy liquid climb the sides.

Breakfast ended when my mother appeared over my shoulder with a comb in one outstretched hand. I stood, thanked her for both the meal and the comb, and then started to groom my head.

Moments later I opened my eyes, realizing I still performed many small, repetitive tasks by feel with eyes shut, and found her standing in front of me with a shiny, polished rock in her hands. It was so shiny it glowed. She handed it to me. I felt its weight, and studied its rigged sides and smooth face.

"Hold it up," she said, and made a gesture with one, open palm, bringing it up to her face.

I did as instructed and was able to watch my jaw drop in my reflection. I blinked a few times to make sure I was seeing what I saw. My dark eyes. The hair I just straightened. My beard surrounding my open mouth. It...I was all there.

For a moment I forgot to breathe. I lowered the rock to see my mother's face replace mine looking back at me, her eyes shiny like the stone, her smile telling a tale of wonder. No words were spoken. It seemed there were no words worth-speaking, nothing that wouldn't break the moment.

I looked back down at the stone, and from a new angle I could see the two dark circles of my nose. My tongue appeared as I wet my lips. My eyes watered and I lost the image as I blinked away the moisture. I regained my composure only to get lost all over again in that amazing rock.

My mother broke my trance by grasping my forearm. "Come. There is one more thing."

Leading me by my arm, she brought me to a weathered chest, residing next to her bedding. Stooping, she opened the chest, and retrieved a neat looking and folded garment. She held it up by the shoulders, letting it unfold towards the floor. "It's your fathers'. It's what men should wear when attending temple gatherings."

I was stunned. Both her forethought and consideration were such a change from last night's silence and tension. "Mother..."

"Arm", she said, holding out one sleeve. It was what she always said when helping me dress. This was the first time I saw her say it, see her hold the garment I was supposed to don and watch the sleeve swallow my hand.

The robe was old, like its owner, but well maintained. No stitch was out of place. My mother stepped behind me and smoothed my shoulders as I looked down at myself, wrapped in this dignified cloak.

I turned back to the table and started to move towards the mirrored stone. I was anxious to see what I would look like to those who awaited me. As I did, mother moved towards the door.

As my hand closed around the rock my mother said, "All right, it's time now." I turned with the stone in hand to see her hands holding the door open while looking back at me. I hastened to lift the stone high enough to sneak a peek at part of my appearance. The garment, with its color of the darkening sky, added a hint of sophistication to both my look and spirit.

I wanted to continue playing with the mirror stone all day, but my brother was waiting to take me to other people in waiting. Replacing my new favorite toy onto the table, I headed out. Mother was now leaning half way out of the house, gesturing to my brother that I was coming.

She turned back around and I noticed her cheeks were flush, like they were just stained by something small and round. She exhaled in a way that told me she was nervous. Reaching out to touch one of her soft shoulders, I said, "Thank you. Thank you for, everything." My other hand was rubbing my overcoat to try and compensate for my bumbling speech.

"I'll be here when you get back," she replied in a soothing way. The thought of 'getting back' was a good one. I felt no nervousness at all until I knew it was time to go.

Mother pulled the door all the way open and I stepped out, into the brightening day. As I did, I inhaled, filling my lungs and raising my chest and shoulders. I was eager to present the new and improved me to my brother.

An invisible fist knocked the wind right out of me when I saw a complete stranger standing where my brother was supposed to be. It took me a moment to resume breathing. My jaw swung down and up, like a shutter in the breeze, but I couldn't make any words come out. I turned back to the house to see my mother peering out at me while she was pushing the door closed.

Her eyes, two wide circles receding into the house, locked on mine. She nodded and removed a hand from the door long enough to make a pushing gesture at me. "Go," she mouthed. I turned back to face my escort. The sound of the door thumping shut told me I was cut off from any further assistance.

He was a little taller than me, even though he stood with his weight shifted towards the road and his head cocked, like he was seeing some new thing for the first time. Dark eyes peered out from deep sockets, cloaked and guarded by darker, thorny brows. Those eyes told me they didn't like what they were seeing.

My hands went cold and my legs locked in place, any change in the wind would have knocked me over. However, the wind, like my mother and brother, vacated the premises. So I continued to just stay frozen.

It was the stranger that moved first. With slow, deliberate steps, he turned to the road while his penetrating eyes commanded me to follow. Once his back was to me, I saw his cropped black hair dangle just above the collar of his earth-colored overcoat.

Before I realized it, I took a few, uncoordinated steps without falling down. I felt the air start to move again. My heart pounded away inside me as if it was trying to catch up with something.

Once upon the road my legs gathered strength. Both my walking and my breathing fell into a pattern. My escort stayed twenty paces ahead of me as we moved in the direction of the city and its heart, the Temple. He seemed to want to avoid conversation as much as I did.

Every couple minutes I would turn to look back at the house I just left. I was perplexed at how things looked different sizes depending my distance from them. Each time I stopped to observe my shrinking homestead so did my escort. Even though he wasn't looking at me, he sensed when I stopped and started, and he followed suit.

My escort's legs dropped to the ground with a heavy, deliberate gate. As I hobbled and shuffled along after him, I studied the sandal marks he left behind in the dirt.

In contrast my steps were short and unsteady. Seeing the ground before me was no help to my feet yet. They were still used to tiptoeing along, waiting to be tripped up by strange obstacles. It was going to take more time before I walked like a seeing person.

We descended a little as the road followed a line of trees and then the house was gone from site. My soul felt like it finally let go of something solid. I felt alone. I pacified myself by focusing on the trees, the scrubby bushes with their pointy shaped leaves and the occasional flowering weed along the road.

My guide broke his silence with a harsh clearing of his throat. From the tree he was passing came hundreds of birds I never knew were there. It was as though the tree shed its leaves at once. With an enraged shriek they departed to the sky, carrying off with them my breath and leaving their former perch a dark and sparse post.

I stood paralyzed with arms up to the sky in defense, my throat and chest locked shut. My eyes were both fascinated and terrified to see for the first time birds in flight. What looked like a chaotic cloud soon shifted into a graceful line that snaked across the sky, beyond more trees and out of vision.

Relaxing and dropping my hands back to my sides, I closed my eyes to listen to the birds for another moment before they were too far away for even that. I was no stranger to bird sounds and I knew birds were able to "jump into the sky for a whole day," as one of my brothers once instructed, but until that moment I didn't know what that looked like.

I opened my eyes to see my guide also looking skyward. He spit something large to the ground, then he resumed his march down the road without any regard for me. I followed, wondering what else was in store for me around the next bend.

I thought about my parents and brothers. If I saw them at that moment, I don't know if I would have screamed at them or clung to them. They abandoned me.

The fear and anger messed my breathing pattern up and I labored to continue down that path. My tunic was wet with my perspiration and my legs felt heavy.

I looked up to see my guide stealing a glance in my direction. His eyes narrowed when they met mine and then widened as he turned away. Without any words between us, I was certain we shared a similar, dark mood.

A while later I heard the distinct timber of metal, probably copper. Looking to my right, I made out a field through the tree line. Several light-colored goats huddled at their shepherd's coaxing. Others seemed to be moving towards him as he waved an arm, holding whatever was making the metallic sounds. Seeing these images though the brush and around the tree trunks made me realize how my vision was sharpening.

That lightened my heart and my lungs could then hold a little more air. The sun was also climbing higher above us and it pleased me more to not have to blink at the brightness. My eyes were growing more confident. Yes indeed, I thought I was going to stay a seeing person.

That thought birthed another one. The reason for all this commotion was *because* I was going to stay a seeing person. The world's plan was to keep kicking me for the rest of my life. I wasn't supposed to ever get off that mat. As much as people didn't like me polluting the public areas, they were not prepared to have me join them in all their hustle and bustle.

Even my family didn't know what to make of it. Instead of celebrating they were hiding and sending me off, alone, to Heaven knows what. If I never made it back home, would they come looking for me? Would they grieve or just bathe in an awkward sense of relief?

My tunic grew hotter but it wasn't because of the sun. My mood was generating the heat. Any anxiety felt over my morning appointment was falling away like sifted sand in one's hand. I still did not know what to make of my silent traveling companion; he was someone to be careful around. But the people I was about to meet were no longer a threat in my mind.

They could throw their weight around with people like my parents. My parents had things to lose. I, on the other hand, had everything to gain with my sight. There were countless things in store for my eyes. My life going forward would be better than blind begging, no matter what happened to me.

Besides, it was understood from our last conversation that I was not their target. They wanted Jesus. My eyes were just some of his handy-work.

Lost in thought and burning with emotion, I did not realize how my walking seemed to level out. My stride took on a steady pace some time after I saw the herd of goats. My legs didn't swing like how my counterpart moved, but I wasn't skipping with hesitation anymore.

I too wanted to ask the man named Jesus a few questions. Why did he choose me? How did he know what to do? Was I ever going to see him again? And last but not least, what was I supposed to tell others that asked me those same questions?

It wasn't long after my walking got better that the road widened. The weeds, grass and brush became scarce. Our feet were no longer kicking up brown clouds of dust that swirled around our ankles. The road turned hard, rocky and worn from years of traffic.

We passed a wood cart being pulled by an ass, traveling back in the direction we came. The man holding the straps around the donkey's head looked up to greet us. My guide didn't return the gesture and his indifference prompted the man to look back at the road without much regard for me.

Up ahead, I could see the high city walls. Their shadows fell away from our direction because the sun was now over our shoulders. More people moved in and out of the gateway to Jerusalem, eager to start their day.

My guide (or guard) shortened the distance between us in an effort to keep us together. *Wouldn't want me to get lost,* I thought. He got close enough to step all over my own shadow as we entered the city. He still seemed to stop and start with me as I looked around, thus becoming in my mind, my *new* shadow.

Watching his feet move, I became fixated on the stone road. How many stones made up this city? How many men worked on it? How many days were spent creating the ground we walked on?

And how many times did I travel this very area, unaware of what was before me? I used to feel the rocks' smooth edges under my feet, as my family brought me to my spot each day. Now I could see the many shades of color in them, and admire the surface they provided.

There were sections where the stones ended and we made our way along dirt and sandy stretches before picking up the stone work again. My feet used to have the journey from my home's threshold to Siloam's pool memorized. However, using eyes instead of toes to navigate left me confused. I couldn't remember if this was the route I took with my brothers yesterday. Everything was starting to feel foreign.

Around a corner we made our appearance on a busier street. There was movement in all directions of people and carts, along with animals and familiar smells of a market's awakening. Two men wearing thick, dark breastplates cut between us for a moment before moving off to our left. They were engrossed in their conversation and did not make eye contact. Their speech disclosed their Roman heritage.

My shadow turned and flashed me a look of caution. He didn't like having someone between us. For a heartbeat or two I was beyond his reach and I could see that frustrated him.

He corralled his composure and pretended to be interested in something on the ground while waiting for me to take another step. Satisfied with me back within reach, he moved forward towards our intended destination, the Temple. I knew from the odors surrounding us we were getting close. Years of blood sacrifice and burnt offerings produced smells throughout the Temple vicinity that were permanent and immovable.

Stairs posed the next challenge. We entered the mouth of a large opening of a stone wall that extended far as I could see in both directions. Once through, we came to a couple sections of cut stone steps, darkened from years of use, which elevated pedestrians to the Temple level of the city. I stood at first, now certain that I did not travel this way yesterday and wondering how I would manage without the strong and steadying arms of my brothers.

The answer I found was one step at a time. My form was not quite a crawl, but also not quite anything else I could describe. Lunging forward, I would seize each step with both hands while bringing my legs up under me to support the next reach. My Shadow Guide stayed by my side, studying my technique with a now-familiar emotional detachment.

Half way up the ascent, I stopped to catch my breath and get my bearings. Shadow looked skyward, then behind us in the direction we came, before uttering his first of just two words to me, "Move."

We soon came to the next flight of cut rock. It was larger and crested at the Temple courtyard. Each step was dark and cool to the touch. The same stone made the waist high walls at each edge, riddled with lines and spots, crevices and bumps. I looked up and watched Shadow head up. Dirt came off his sandals, adding to the stones' darker parts.

He leaned to the right as he went, his right leg bent easier than his left and at once he appeared older than me. He was almost to the top and sensed I wasn't as close to him as he would like. He looked back at me with those dark, penetrating eyes and grunted, "Come."

It was my turn. Both legs twitched a little, still not sure which should go first. My left pushed forward and my heel pressed hard on the first step, planting itself. My hips rocked and up came the right leg. I did it. No crawling required! I stood squarely on that first step, both happy one was done and a bit overwhelmed at all that remained.

After two more awkward steps, I shifted to my right, reaching for the short wall. The smooth, dimpled texture of the wall brought

53

some perspective to my efforts. I allowed myself to hang there a moment with eyes shut. I made my way up the rest of the flight, alternating between eyes opened and closed, my right hand leading the way on the half-wall.

I got my first taste of victory, ever, when I reached the stairs' summit. A little out of breath, my heart hammered in my ears, and I forgot for a moment where I was headed. Shadow avoided eye contact now, more comfortable that I was on the Temple grounds. He looked around me, instead of directly at me, before resuming his walk towards the Temple's major structures.

What looked like a small, distant mountain when we entered the city, now stood enormous before me. I followed Shadow as he walked towards an entryway that seemed taller than some of the trees we passed outside the city walls. It was a gateway to an expansive courtyard. It looked as though the courtyard was large enough to hold the entire city and was surrounded with a parameter of columns and wide, covered hallways. The odors I smelled as we approached the Temple were now thick, pungent.

Many windows were cut into the walls of those covered hallways and I gathered there were lots of rooms and chambers in this city-within-a-city. Through the gateway and to the right, Shadow moved without hesitation. He stopped at the third door and knocked with one hand while pushing it open with the other.

- 9 -

Still a few steps behind, I saw deep inside the room. The men from yesterday, the Pharisees that questioned me, were several lengths away, breaking off a conversation to eye me. A few others moved about the room, busy with tasks and not very interested with us. I could tell they were working to ensure things were set for our meeting that was about to begin.

The room quieted as two of the men took seats behind a table, and the third, the heavy-set one, moved forward to greet me. Skinny, the agitated one from yesterday interlaced boney fingers as he settled into his chair and pursed his mouth.

The heavy one smiled wide, "Give God the praise." He shot a look backwards to his companions I did not understand, but the air in the room told me he was amused with himself. *Give God the Praise?* That's what my father would say to my brothers when they were not doing what they were told. It usually meant *act right,* or *tell the truth!*

Turning back to me, his eyebrows raised up as he spied my attire. He looked me up and down and gestured with open, plump hands at my father's cloak. He repeated his greeting, a little slower, "Give God the Praise." *Heavy,* as I thought to name him at that moment, got so close to me I could smell him - a little garlic and a lot of soap, the kind rich people used. Its sweetness enveloped his space, and announced his invasion of mine.

"We know that this man is a sinner." Heavy shifted his weight back from me and stared. That was it, no "thank you for coming back," no "help us understand a point you made yesterday", just... "answer Us."

Annoyed, I stepped into his pregnant pause, "If he is a sinner, I do not know. One thing I do know is that I was blind and now I see." *In more ways than one* I thought, but I didn't go that far. They looked at each other and for the first time since putting on my father's coat that morning, I felt sure and steady inside.

I can't say I had a plan on how to handle this meeting, but now that the immovable fact of my eyesight was placed before every one, and I noticed how it caused my interrogators to hesitate, I decided to stay with it and not budge. With his back to me, Heavy bent over, as if exasperated, and rested his meaty hands on the table his partners faced.

I re-surveyed the room and was disappointed the older, more reasonable Pharisee from yesterday was not present. I wondered if that was on purpose.

Heavy bobbed his large head and slammed a fist on the table, making his thick, shiny hair bounce as he swirled back around to me. "What did he do to you?" he bellowed. "*How* did he open your eyes?"

This was incredible. They had no interest in anything I had to share because it wasn't what they wanted, but they were going to persist with all the same questions already asked multiple times. The only thing left to be revealed was who would be more mule-like, them or me.

It was my turn to raise my voice. "I told you already and you did not listen." Surprise splashed across Heavy's face. "Why do you want to hear it again? Do you want to become his disciples too?"

Skinny jumped out of his chair, "You are that man's disciple; we are disciples of Moses!" He gestured back and forth to his colleagues with those long, pointy fingers. Heavy's face was changing, tensing up. Skinny man continued, "We know that God spoke to Moses, but we do not know where this one is from."

How can that even be, I thought. I answered, "This is what is so amazing, that you do not know where he is from, yet he opened my eyes. We know that God does not listen to sinners, but if one is devout and does his will, he listens to him."

I think my utterance of God's name enraged Heavy more. I felt heat coming from him at me like the sun. Unfazed, I wanted to make one more point. "It is unheard of that anyone ever opened the eyes of a person born blind." My hands came up and touched my cheeks. I looked Skinny right in his eyes, "If this man were not from God, he would not be able to do anything."

With that the room erupted like a sudden thunderstorm. The quiet one who sat next to Skinny threw his arms up in the air, Heavy exhaled and let out a half moan. Skinny grabbed his vestments and grimaced. He outstretched an arm and launched a finger at me that resembled a spear tip, his voice was shrill, "You were born totally in sin, and you are trying to teach us?" His other hand still clung to his garments near his heart.

Heavy found the word he was looking for. "Out!" is what I remember him yelling just before the blows came from my morning's escort, my Shadow. I saw inside Heavy's open mouth that spit forth his indignation. His teeth were straight and whiter than any I'd seen yet. They were what I imagined bones looked like.

Shadow attacked from his perch to my right, where moments before he leaned against a thick, ornate table. His closed fist landed on the side of my head, not very hard, but it did steal my breath as I reeled back, in a futile attempt to get away from him. His other hand grabbed my cloak, my father's cloak, up near my throat.

I shrunk in his clutches as my left knee buckled. I crumpled as he pulled my cloak up around my face. The sound of heavy wood sliding across the stone floor erupted, as the meeting's other attendees moved at once for a better view.

"..him outta here!", Heavy spat as Shadow struggled for a better grip. Blows thumped down on my back. I bowed my head further into my father's cloak that was still under arrest in Shadow's clutch. The punches glanced off, many just missing a solid landing along my ribs and around my shoulders and back. Shadow's fury poured out of him and he gurgled as he continued to swing at me. Unsatisfied with his angle of assault, he shifted his weight without letting me go. He positioned himself directly behind me and kicked my tailbone hard!

The cloak, which was pulled tight around my neck, loosened enough that my head pulled free as I rocked from the kick. Both Shadow and I looked at each other, stunned, realizing at the same instant that he'd pulled my cloak off me and I was then free of his grasp.

While my mind remained frozen my body shuttered and fled. With Shadow and the rest of the room behind me and the door before me, I grabbed and pulled the door halfway open before even formulating a rational thought.

Realizing his prize was about to escape, Shadow lunged forward, cloak still in hand, and landed around my waist. The cloak was still bunched up in one fist, so he could not secure me. Even though I stumbled and my forehead bounced hard off the open door, I wiggled free of him. For a second, I saw a bright flicker in my head, behind closed eyes, as pain blossomed above my eyebrows.

Bursting through the opening, my throat and lungs reopened and I heard myself scream. My legs moved faster than I ever remember them moving, as they tried to catch up to the rest of me. I didn't dare look up until I was halfway across the courtyard.

I knew Shadow was behind me, closing in. I felt his footsteps and looked back. As I turned, my feet collided and down I went. The ground jumped up at me fast and my left shoulder and ear stopped it cold. I screamed again.

I rolled onto my back and put my hands out, to block Shadow-

I was alone. I saw Shadow standing in the entrance to the room I just fled. He turned his back to me and went in, closing the door behind him.

My chest heaved up and down and could not be controlled. After a few moments I became aware of some other people, moving about the courtyard at a safe distance. I looked down at myself, and noticed dark spots on the left sleeve and on my front under my chin. My ear throbbed and I was slow to touch it. It hurt and felt wet. Seeing blood for the first time on my fingers, running down into my palm, explained the stains on my clothes.

The first complete thought I remember having, after telling myself to get up, was *what now?* My father's cloak was gone. They took it. Holy men?! Curse them! My father would finish what Shadow started when he found out. That was, if I could even make it home on my own. *What now?*

- 10 -

My heart and breathing slowed as I looked in all directions, across the massive courtyard, trying to choose a direction to walk. I got my bearings and took the first of many hopeful steps, towards a more welcoming place.

Once at the bottom of the steps I stopped again, looking at the way I thought I came, but also seeing the street as though for the first time. More people and activity in all directions made everything seem new and a fresh wave of confusion hit.

Closing my eyes for immediate retreat, I'm almost ashamed to admit I wished to go back and sit by the pool, to figure things out. I shook my head at the irony - Here I was, with the ability to walk freely where and when I wanted, my life's dream, but I stood still, afraid to move.

The thought of my mother provided the needed motivation. She could help, and she was waiting for me. I could think of her pacing about, worrying. I needed to get back to her and explain what they did. And I needed to arrive home before my father!

With this new goal at the center of my attention, I set out. I found my way back to the city gates and onto the road with the trees and fields where earlier, I saw the shepherds working. They were no longer there but I remembered the view. The hills were now before me, and somewhere amongst them was our village.

The walk was slow and I kept looking back as I made my way, both interested in seeing the city look smaller and making sure Shadow wasn't closing in behind, with more blood on his mind.

I walked and walked, sometimes stopping to second guess myself. My mind eased when I came to a small rise, and the road went up through some trees. I remembered walking that way before, and seeing the city off in the distance from the crest of the little hill that morning, as I emerged from those same trees. Home was getting closer.

Up I went and then turned to look back. The city was bright on the horizon, bathed in sunlight. I felt somewhat proud that I made it so far on my own, and allowed myself to enjoy the view for another moment.

The sound of sandals on the road came up behind me. I shuddered as I turned to see a man moving along with the help of a long stick. His eyes were set on mine but I did not recognize him. Not knowing what I should do, I looked down at my own sandals and just remained still, letting him make his way.

I listened to his movements but still did not recognize him as one of my neighbors. There was a steady, sluggish rhythm coming from both his feet and stick as he walked. When he was almost past me, I ventured another glance up at his face and saw him still looking out of the corners of his eyes at me. My hand moved to my face in a self conscious effort to determine the man's interest, and felt the lump on my forehead.

My fingertips gently explored my ear, still tender and stinging to the touch. I then looked at the dark stains on my tunic and had a pretty good idea why the man examined me so. I turned away, now looking in the direction of home. The village was there, still a ways off, but visible.

My legs felt new energy. I could make it home to my mother. I kept on, making little clouds of dust with my feet.

Getting closer and closer, the village started to look and sound more alive. People were outside their homes, working and interacting. Their sounds were muted but growing louder. Some little puffs of smoke, from family ovens outside and behind dwellings, swirled and climbed above the tops of fences and roofs.

Two boys came running from the village, heading in my direction. They were talking as they ran and I could tell they were in their own little world. The first of the boys looked twice at me as he passed and the second didn't look up at all.

My home was the second on the right, along the village's border. I moved at almost a run myself, stumbling along, trying to watch both the road and the houses. So close to the finish, I didn't want to repeat my fall from the Temple courtyard.

My neighbor saw me first. She called out to my mother, who had joined her at their oven. They must have been sharing the wood and maybe even some of the ingredients to do the day's baking.

Mother turned, ran, and met me on the road. Her hands were raised and shaking, she looked me up and down, not knowing where to touch me first.

"What happened?!"

"They took it. They took the coat!" I croaked through sudden tears. She grabbed my shoulders and pulled me after her, as she headed towards the house. She sat me down on a stool outside our home and she scurried to get some water and a rag.

My ear flowered with fresh pain as she cleaned off the dried blood. She tried to console me by taking on some of my burden. "I'm sorry son. I should've never agreed to you going off on your own."

I met her eyes and noticed fresh creases around them. "What do we do now?"

Not sure if either of us believed her, but she responded with a curt, "It's going to be fine." She finished wiping my head and hands down, brought me some water to drink, then moved me inside.

Once in a fresh tunic, I sat on a cushion, now on the other side of the same wall I was against as Mother cleaned me up. The room was dark and cool. My backside throbbed and my shoulder reminded me of my graceful exit from the Temple meeting room. My head pounded.

I heard sounds outside, Mother conversing with neighbors, women's voices, and after some time I dozed off. Awhile later I snapped awake. My hearing was still my most developed sense, and the sounds of whom my mother spoke to changed; the sounds were deeper, masculine.

Stiff as the wall itself, I kept my eyes closed and focused my whole being into those sounds. Was it him? Was my father home, learning of my, his loss?

There were no signs of agitation. I heard my mother say "Yes, he is here, but not available now." Not *available*. Her tone was matter-of-fact. No, she was not talking to Father.

I got to my feet and ventured a peek from the closest window. Through a crack in the shutters I saw someone walking away from her and our lot. He was young, younger than I. Never saw him before. *Now what's going on?* Do they really want to abuse me more? I examine him the best I could. He didn't carry around the same darkness as my morning Shadow, and his dress did not proclaim Pharisee. From what I saw, he seemed, normal.

Mother came in next, holding fresh baked bread wrapped in her apron. The fragrance brought my stomach alive. The events of my day put my body through much and I realized I was starving. She noticed my interest and as she turned to leave again, said, "Just one."

So warm, dark and crisp on the edges, that bread was the best part of my day. Back to my cushion, I ate with eyes closed, allowing myself to forget about my father for a bit.

He couldn't be forgotten forever though, and as the daylight in the room diminished, he did return. Like our last visitor, I heard his voice from a distance. He and my mother were farther away, the sound of him yelling brought me to attention. I had a hard time making out what was said. Random sounds from both of them, parts of words and the raising and lowering of their voices were all I could make out. I could tell Mother went to meet him on the road.

Then there were footsteps, the sound of something heavy slammed down outside our door. One of my father's tools clanged against the wall. I heard one of his loud exhales. "He inside?" he asked in a lower tone.

The next voice to jump in was that of my older brother. A short sound, just loud enough to announce his appearance.

Mother came in and started grabbing things from around the pantry. Wine and cups. The bread. A container of olives. She filled one cup and left it on the table along with another piece of bread and a dish of olives. The rest was scooped up, along with a few other dishes and out she went, to serve her husband and son.

The message, though not spoken, was loud and clear. I was not invited and would be dining alone this evening. Fine. She was doing me a favor, and she probably knew it.

After slipping over to the table to retrieve my meal, I moved back to the wall so I could try listening.

It was quiet for a while until the sound of my younger brother presented itself. Mother served him and then conversation began. Interesting, I thought. A family meeting about me, without me. My brothers were most likely going to eat twice tonight. Here, and then again with their own families.

My mother said something and was answered by my younger brother. "No Mother, Father is right."

Next to chime in was my older brother, "So where's he gonna go?"

After a moment, my father mumbled something, probably through a mouthful. Then I heard, "Y'know, they have plenty of space."

They're sending me somewhere. Fear and relief both struggled for dominance in my heart. Someplace else meant getting away from people that beat you for telling the truth, and leaving the tension that filled this home. But it also meant being in places I knew not and yet another journey, alone without my mother close by.

Mother said something that sounded like an objection, to which my father responded, "He's never known that work, and couldn't keep up."

Not long after, I heard mother collecting the dishes. Their discussion was concluded and mother started bringing things inside. The others left, my brothers off to their own homes and father off to anywhere away from me.

She came in and busied herself with the clean up. Her back was to me when I asked, "Where am I going now?"

Her shoulders dropped and she hesitated before turning to reply, "Your uncle's place in Bethany, just until things settle down."

Bethany was another village on the other side of the city. I looked away and mother continued to straighten the pantry and clean the dishes. Afterwards, she brought me my mattress in a roll and then started packing up a few of my things. It looked like I would be leaving right away.

I couldn't help myself and quipped, "Who's going to show up to escort me next?" As soon as the words left my lips I was sorry. Mother looked up as if I hit her. I'm not sure who shed the first tear but we both were sobbing before long.

I went to her, expecting to be slapped in return, but she hugged me tighter than I ever remember. We both apologized again and again to each other, and I hung onto her shoulders just keep my balance. My legs felt weak and my shoulders jerked up and down as I tried to control my breathing. After a few more moments, she coaxed me back over to my mattress. Even in her pain, she could still keep things moving along, in her persistent, quiet way.

I just wanted that day to end! Not longer after, I fell asleep and dreamt of me sitting again back in my spot by the pool, begging. I was a seeing beggar in the dream, and examined all who passed. I saw all the looks of disapproval on those faces, until some men in Pharisee's clothing strutted by, smiling and nodding. I blinked and then was sitting at the water's edge, staring into the water at the reflection of my own eyes. They seemed so bright and wide against the darkened pool. In my reflection I saw the rest of my face and head, covered in mud. In fact, in the dream I understood I was made of mud, a mud man, except for those bright eyes. They were like two star lights in the night sky.

- 11 -

I've always had trouble with my days and nights, and things have been no different since getting my sight. Usually I would hear my parents' sleep sounds to know it was still 'night time'. These past two nights when I've come awake, I've enjoyed the peace of the darkness. It's given me time to put things in perspective.

Waking from a seeing dream is quite different from experiencing a sound and sensation dream. I looked at my hands in the darkness and rubbed them together. No dirt or mud present, just skin. Those dream images were still fresh, as fresh as any of my memories from yesterday's action.

Like always, in time I drifted off again until morning. Before that time I kept thinking of those two starry eyes, my starry eyes, and the light coming from them.

I woke again to the sounds of my Mother moving about. With eyes only half open I could tell she was busy preparing me (and herself) for my departure. She was in the pantry and when she moved to the table I saw her tying up some food in a cloth, food for the journey I suspected. It was morning and my father was already gone.

After getting up and cleaning up, I stared at myself in the bowl of water. A much cleaner face than last night's dream looked back at me and I decided that looking at my reflection was my new favorite thing. My left ear looked bigger than the right.

My thoughts were interrupted with sounds of conversation coming from outside. I peered out. I expected to see a few neighbors, but instead saw a small crowd coming down the road towards our village. My mouth dropped open when I realized the group was being led by Jesus. What was he doing here? He was walking and talking with a younger, shorter man. The others filled out the road and formed a swaying tail to the path Jesus and his companion made.

I couldn't be sure, but the tunic of the younger man reminded me of the person that stopped by our house yesterday and spoke with my mother. Mother happened to be out front and she came into view. Like me, she stopped, stood alert but still as Jesus and his group made a direct course for our home.

The young man said something to Jesus and motioned to my mother. Jesus nodded and placed his hand on the young man's shoulder, stopping him short. He then proceeded towards mother alone. The rest of the group settled in around the younger man at our property's edge and watched.

The crowd was made up of both men and women, young and old, rich and poor. Most of the men dressed like me and my family, working class. A group of them gathered together next to the younger man Jesus spoke to. The others were content to fall in behind them. A couple nicer dressed individuals, with richer looking robes resembling Temple-types, stood a couple *pedes* closer to Jesus. They leaned forward, trying not to miss a word.

Mother stood her ground in the presence of the crowd. She appeared stiff, and ready to give someone a tongue lashing. That stance changed as soon as Jesus addressed her. He looked right at her, tilted his head a little and smiled. I saw his lips move but couldn't make out the words. It was then I realized I was free to move closer. Why hide in the house when the very person I wished to meet the most was right there?

I came out into the light and Jesus looked up, his eyes meeting mine. There was that same calmness in his gaze I first saw at the pool, when everyone else was storming around me and my new eyes. He stepped in my direction and mother let him pass. All eyes were on us, but I didn't feel pressured or uncomfortable from the attention. For the first time ever amongst strangers, I didn't feel like I was being judged by the on-lookers.

Jesus grasped both my arms, firm but not harmful, almost at shoulder height. He looked at my eyes, both in and around them, like he was inspecting his work or checking them for something specific.

Just then, two of the men that were grouped around Jesus' younger friend separated and my father stepped through. He walked towards us and stopped for a moment, staring at Jesus. He then continued, in silence, to the house. I heard the door close behind me.

Jesus blinked and shifted his gaze a little, not really looking at me but more looking into me. He spoke and surprised me with his choice of words. "Do you believe in the Son of Man?"

Son of Man!?! It took me a moment to understand what I heard. Son of Man I learned about as a boy. Mother told me stories from the synagogue readings and I hadn't thought of that phrase in a long time. The Son of Man was a just ruler to come over all the land; he partnered with Yahweh. An image I never saw before came to me of such a king we could see, meet and befriend.

I was ready for a Son of Man at that time, in our land. "Who is he, sir, that I may believe in him?"

Without hesitation, Jesus replied with eyebrows raised, "You have seen him, and the one speaking to you now is he." The words splashed over me and despite his humble appearance, I knew they were true. Everything and everyone else washed away. Here was the ruler of Everlasting Dominion, visiting *me*! He healed *me*! He came back for *me*! For reasons beyond comprehension, he wanted *me*!

The air rushed out of me, "I do believe, Lord."

Without knowing, my legs took it upon themselves to buckle and I dropped to the ground, still clinging to his clothes, his hands still on my arms, and I bowed to this Son of Man. A few murmurs, oohs and ahhs sprung from the crowd and I imagined my shocked family running and hiding. That thought amused me. My free expression would embarrass them, but my action felt natural and appropriate. I could see unlike ever before, all because of the Just One before me.

Jesus let the moment pass, then guided me back to my feet, his hands still on my arms. He half turned to his followers and raised a finger at them.

"I came into this world for judgment, so that those who do not see might see, and those who *do* see might become blind."

I searched the crowd, and looked at faces. Some appeared happy, some looked confused at what was just said, some just stared at Jesus, waiting on each next word. The two dressed like Pharisees looked at each other. One then spoke up, with a crinkled brow and asked, "Surely we are not also blind, are we?" With his hands he gestured to himself and his partner.

Jesus reset his footing, faced the crowd all the way and addressed the two men that questioned him? "If you were blind, you would have no sin." He waved his finger.

No sin? I thought. People told me all my life that I was full of sin.

Jesus continued, "But now you are saying, 'We see', so, your sin remains."

They looked stunned and remained still for a moment. A bird cried off in the distance. It was the only sound that filled the void. Jesus scanned the whole crowd, and even nodded in my mother's direction, then continued, "Amen, amen, I say to you, whoever does not enter a sheepfold through the gate but climbs over elsewhere is a thief and a robber.

"But whoever enters through the gate is the shepherd of the sheep. The gatekeeper opens it for him, and the sheep hear his voice, and he calls his own sheep by name and leads them out. When he has driven out all his own, he walks ahead of them, and the sheep follow him, because they recognize his voice."

I marveled at his teaching and how he turned a question into a lesson. Our home front became an open air synagogue. It was his speech, and the way he held everyone's attention, that made him appear as the King I now thought him to be.

"But they will not follow a stranger," he said as he stepped a little in the direction of the two that questioned him. "They run away from him, because they do not recognize the voice of strangers."

A couple of the followers sat down on the ground, got comfortable. They read signals from Jesus I did not notice, or knew his style better than the rest. Their attempt to relax started to spread. More of the group settled down as Jesus continued. A young couple moved closer to me. A girl with shiny hair looked at me and smiled wide, from both her mouth and her eyes. Her companion also nodded and smiled. They took their seats near me.

Jesus paused, looked around, then began again. "Amen, amen, I say to you, I am the gate for the sheep." He brought his hands in to touch his chest. "All who came before me are thieves and robbers, but the sheep did not listen to them. I am the gate. Whoever enters through me will be saved, and will come in and go out and find pasture."

I am the gate. That phrase hung in my mind.

"A thief only comes to steal and slaughter and destroy; I came so that they could have life and have it more abundantly. I am the good shepherd. A good shepherd lays down his life for the sheep." More heads nodded now.

I saw my brothers standing just beyond those sitting in front of the house, or more specifically, in front of Jesus. A few neighbors started gathering as well. Still others I could see looking on from their own home fronts, or peering out from open shutters and doors.

"A hired man, who is not a shepherd and whose sheep are not his own, sees a wolf coming and leaves the sheep and runs away, and the wolf catches and scatters them. This is because he works for pay and has no concern for the sheep.

"I am the good shepherd, and I know mine and mine know me; just as the Father knows me and I know the Father; and I will lay down my life for the sheep.

He then turned, surveyed the villagers listening in and restarted, loud enough for all to hear. "I have other sheep that do not belong to this fold. These also I must lead, and they will hear my voice, and there will be one flock." His finger again came up, this time over his head. "One shepherd."

"This is why the Father loves me, because I lay down my life in order to take it up again. No one takes it from me, but I lay it down on my own." Jesus circled, meeting eyes along the way. "I have the power to lay it down, and the power to take it up again. This command... I have received from my Father."

Jesus looked down at the group sitting on the ground and then spoke quietly to a few of them. The two men in the expensive robes were debating what was said to them. I heard only bits and pieces, but one clearly said, "Why listen to him?" His partner responded and in doing so, motioned in my direction.

Yes, back to me again. Words and their meanings can be debated, contested, discounted, but I cannot. I am here, living, breathing proof of Jesus' goodness. My eyes are all the proof I will ever need now.

That thought brought along another: no more explaining and re-explaining myself to those who do not want to listen. And no more allowing others to treat me as an inconvenience. I know the truth, and I suspect they will as well just by meeting my eyes.

Jesus, my Son of Man, has proven himself to be full of surprises, and I was eager to witness what he had in store for us next. Whatever it was, I knew I would not forget what it looked like! There may come a day for me to travel to my Uncle's land. That day, however, would have to wait. It was the time for me to follow another man's lead, the Son of Man's lead, and I could not think of a better place to be.

...To Be Continued.

My letter to you:

Thank you so very much for reading Eyewitness! What you are holding took me about 15 years to get to you. I could never shake the story idea of what did the blind man actually see after Jesus chose him?, and began writing it many years ago. Over time, in between the day jobs, family commitments and other writings, I kept going back to Eyewitness and pecking away at the keyboard. I often dreamed of this day, when you would hold this story and read this note.

I write for you - whether it's non-fiction or fiction, you are my mission. Because of this, I need to ask you for two things:

1. Could you please leave a review of Eyewitness on Amazon.com? Good or bad, a review is very important in my quest to share Eyewitness with everyone. The more reader reviews are written, the more Amazon will suggest the book to others.
2. If you have any thoughts on Eyewitness that could help me promote it, or advice I could use in writing other books, can

you please email me? I'm at jc@JohnCConnell.com . I look forward to hearing from you and I will keep you up to date on my books, blog and projects!

God Bless,
JC

Please visit:

My Amazon Page Link -
http://www.amazon.com/John-C.-
Connell/e/B009N7UDIK/ref=sr_ntt_srch_lnk_
1?qid=1403988999&sr=8-1

My Site & Blog - http://johncconnell.com

My Facebook Page -

https://www.facebook.com/johncconnellauthor

My Twitter Feed -

https://twitter.com/JohnC_Author